Published by
The Dial Press
1 Dag Hammarskjold Plaza
New York, New York 10017

The work was first published in Great Britain
by Andersen Press Ltd.

Printed in Italy.
First U.S.A. printing.
Design by Atha Tehon

Library of Congress Cataloging in Publication Data
Testa, Fulvio.
If you take a paintbrush.
Summary: Children in and out of doors
are depicted with things of the major colors:
white snow, red apples, brown chocolate, etc.
[1. Color—Fiction] I. Title. II. Series.
PZ7.T2875Ie 1983   [E]   82-45512
ISBN 0-8037-3829-3

The art for each picture consists of an ink
and dye painting, that is camera-separated
and reproduced in full color.

If You Take a Paintbrush
A BOOK OF COLORS
FULVIO TESTA

The Dial Press · New York

Yellow is the color of the sun.

Blue is the color of the sea.

Yellow and blue together make green.

Green is the color of trees in springtime.

Orange is the color of oranges.

Red is the color of apples.
Nicholas's car is red too.

Purple is the color of the sweater Nicholas got for his birthday. Purple is the flower he gives to Nancy.

Brown is the color of chocolate.

Gray is the color of the water when you take a bath.

This cat is black. Black is the color of the night.

White is the color of snow.

White is a piece of paper waiting for colors.

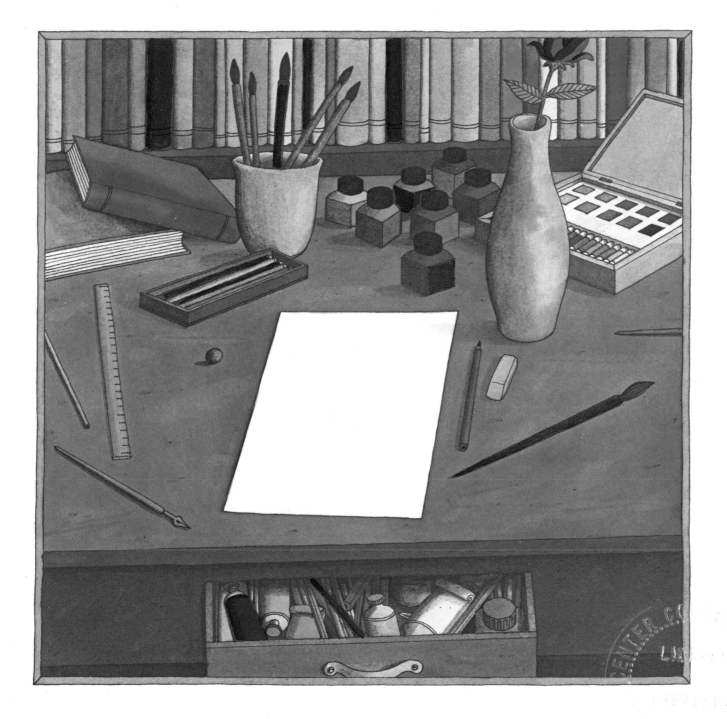